Naked in the Swamp

Naked in the Swamp

Twenty-One Short Stories

Mohammad Saeed Habashi

To order additional copies of this book, contact:
Xlibris
1-888-795-4274
www.Xlibris.com
Orders@Xlibris.com
696629

Contents

Stars of the Port 7

Midnight Customers 15

The Laughing Humpback 25

A Love as Hot as the Summer Heat 35

Thirsty on the Ocean 45

Wounded Snake 49

The Uncle 55

The Rose Offered by the Beloved 59

Solmaz and Saghakhaneh's Candles 63

On the Cobbles of Paris 67

Deep under the Waters of Chao Phraya 73

Thirst at the Seventh Station 81

Naked in the Swamp 87

The Secret of Those Black Eyes 95

Twenty Years of Expectation 101

A Whirlwind Romance at the Seaside 111

Shila 117

Northbound and Southbound Trains 121

Spending a Friday with Gina Lollobrigida 125

A Cup of Black Coffee 129

Darya 135

Stars of the Port

JASEM WOULD LEAVE home for the sea at the crack of dawn day in, day out. His skin was tanned after years of exposure to the brine and the southern scorching sunlight. His straight black hair danced across his wide forehead as the breeze hit them. He was tall and had manly features. Diving had granted him sharp eyes that let him distinguish even the remotest objects on the horizon. Whenever he dived deep into the sea, he wouldn't come back empty-handed. He wouldn't call it a dayunless he'd find at least one pearl among the oysters he had found. An average boat would carry him off the Kong's coast. His muscles and chest had been developed following years of rowing. When he left for Bandar-e 'Abbas or Kuwait for shopping, some folks who didn't know him by sight assumed that he was a bodybuilder.

In a morning, in which the blue waters of the Persian Gulf smoothly touched the sandy beaches of Bandar-e

Kong, Jasem set off for the sea. He was rowing, with his eyes curiously roving over the water, as if he knew what was going on deep inside the sea. His father had taught him how to dive. A shark injured his father when Jasem was twelve. It was almost seven years since the first time he started to go to the sea alone.

His mind, at the same time he was rowing and watching the water, was wandering around. He was waiting for a day on which he managed to dig out a pearl that would be worth a fortune, enough to do up the compact house left by his father and to bring its wind catcher back to life. Also, he wanted to fulfill his mother's wish and marry a girl, which might help him put an end to the habit of looking up at the stars. Consciously or unconsciously, he was looking for the lucky star; however, it didn't stop him from thinking deeply of *khalīfah*'s sister.

Not being far from the beach, he could still see the old and young men busy building ships by the sea. Having rowed farther ahead, he turned his attention to his hunting and finally had his eyes glued to a spot. He pulled the oars back into the boat and stood up to dive.

He had recently bought black underpants on. The shopper reminded him of what Jasem had already known "Sharks fear the black color." His mother passed on her best wishes to the shopper and praised her son to the skies for paying full attention to what the shopper said.

First, he took a look at the sky. He then took a deep breath before plunging into the tranquil waters of the Persian Gulf. All of a sudden, a floating object caught his sight way off. Paying more attention, he managed to recognize the hands of a human being. The scene took his mind off looking for pearls. He rushed to the spot only to see the hands had gone under. Then, he didn't hesitate to dive into the water. After a while, he appeared again on the surface, yet he was not alone anymore, with his arms holding an apparently lifeless young woman in a firm grip. He carried her to the boat.

Night fell. The sea was still quiet. Stars were twinkling overhead. Bandar-e Kong was peacefully sleeping. But Jasem and his mother were keeping a constant vigil by the woman. She came to life again, having the clothes of Jasem's mother on. An oil lamp was shedding light on the curious faces of those three, with their outsized shadows falling on the wall around, but they all were small and silent. The young lady had yet to speak, having no idea of where she was and what she was supposed to say. She might have not felt like saying something. The mother left the room and called the son.

"Go and sleep," she said, adding "Women well understand one another's feelings I will tell you the story in the morning."

Jasem did so, but he couldn't get to asleep. He didn't think about the sea and pearls anymore. He couldn't help focusing his attention on the young lady. It was the first time he had hugged a woman outside the closely knit circle of his family, the first time he had put pressure on the chest of a woman, the first time he had seen the naked legs of a woman and the first time he had put his lips on the lips of another woman. He must have done so, after all, in order to revive her. At that time, he found himself entangled with her. He asked himself hundreds of times by the time dawn broke, "What did a nice lady as young as this do in the sea? "Was she there to be prayed by him?"

At dawn, the mother rose to bake bread for the breakfast.

"She is an aristocrat," told the mother to her son while she was by the tanoor[1] "She is expecting an illegitimate baby, so she wanted to drown herself," she added.

"Who the hell had made her pregnant" Jasem asked her mother surprisingly.

"A boy belonging to her family," replied the mother.

"Fuck such a relative then," shouted Jasem, spitting unintentionally on the ground.

"If I tell you whose daughter she is, you will fly into a temper!"

"Ha! Whose daughter is she?"

"The chief of *Nazmiyeh*.[2]"

"What does she want to do now?" asked Jasem after he unintentionally jumped up, walked nervously around, and clapped his hands on purpose.

"She has no idea yet, but I let her family in on this," replied his mother.

"We shall keep her here. I have fallen in love with her," said Jasem to his mother immediately, as if he had managed to hunt the sought-after oyster with a precious large pearl inside it.

---

[1] A traditional oven dug into the earth used for baking bread.

[2] The name of Iran's police department in the past

"Shut up, watch your language" retorted his mother, looking daggers at him with her eyebrows raised.

What Jasem heard did not catch him by surprise for he was well familiar with his mother's behavior, and also with the local customs of Bandar. He just took a quick look at her and left the house without having breakfast.

Next morning, Jasem was in Bandar-e 'Abbas. When he got off the *motor lanj*[3] and put his feet on the pier, it was almost high noon. *Jashoos*[4] were frying crabs on their motor lanjs. They used empty tins of oil filled with burning coal and ash to fry the crabs, which were grilled alive.

Jasem, with an appetite ruined by their customs, did not feel like having a bite. He also couldn't resign himself to his mother anymore, who once asked him to bite his tongue after he informed his mother of his desire for the Khalifeh's sister. Khalifeh also asked him to further reflect on it, if he was to marry his sister. But never had Jasem contemplated on what they meant by these remarks. After all, he used to spend all his time at sea. Now Jasem was on the way to the Khalifeh's house to tell him he had well thought. Arriving there, he encountered a sealed wooden door with two crossing timbers nailed to it. He surprisingly asked a salesman standing at a nearby stall the reason why the door had been sealed.

"Nazmiyeh has closed it," replied the stall's owner.

---

[3] A kind of boat used for sailing in the Persian Gulf, Oman Sea, and Indian Ocean.

[4] The workers who toil on boats in Southern Iran.

Jasem failed to understand what had happened again. He always likened anything to oysters, which offered a circular pearl whenever opened. Now he let the thought of the sea and pearls go, behaving like lovers. He wanted to deny himself the desire for touching the limbs of the young woman by tracking down his first love. He sought the Khalifeh's sister through his eyes with his mind forming a picture of the thighs, chest, and anything belonging to the woman whose life he had saved.

Asking for the direction from those going along, he managed to find Khalifeh's place, one farsang[5] from Bandar-e 'Abbas, being called Shaghu[6].

Love seemed to have driven him out of his mind. When he gave the residents the signs and asked for direction, he failed to pay attention to their questioning looks.

Kalifeh was surprised when he faced Jasem.

"I am here to tell you I have come down in favor of marrying your sister."

Speechless Kalifeh invited him to sit on a flat wooden couch. There was a straw mat on the couch and another one was being hung from a date palm, wetted to let the wind carry a gentle, cool breeze to the people resting on the couch; it cooled Jasem down too. He then asked Khalifeh for the whereabouts of his sister. Having been stunned by the question, he pointed to a room by moving his head.

---

[5] A unit for measuring distance equal to 3.75 miles.

[6] The place where the whores stay (a red light district)

"She will come out in a few minutes," he replied.

In a few minutes, Zahra came out, with a traditional *neghab*[7] on. She got disarticulated at the sight of Jasem. Having his eyes glued to her, Jasem made a comparison between her contours, covered by a greenish - red dress stretching from the top to her legs, and those of the woman he saved. Jasem's face lit up, which pacified Zahra. She walked slowly toward him, with small silver and copper bells fastened around her ankles jingling and clanging. They made Jasem find his heart pounding.

Hardly had he calmed down when a man left the room. He was fastening his belt. Jasem sprang to his feet after catching a glimpse of him, and he rushed away.

From then on, nobody saw Jasem.

---

[7] A veil worn by some traditional women in Southern Iran.

Midnight Customers

GRAY CLOUDS HIGH in the sky burst into rain as he began to leave Karaj. A wiper was out of order. Luckily, it was on the passenger side; otherwise, he would have been in no condition to drive in such rainy weather. Not only was he looking at the road ahead, he was also keeping a close eye on the cars driving close behind. Once a light traveled its way through the misty space of the vehicle, his eyes began to scan the incoming traffic to learn whether he was being chased along or not. As any car overtook him and spun indifferently past, the expression on his face suggested he was thankful to God.

He was at the wheel of a rattletrap Opel coupe, sluggishly rolling up a sloping road leading off Karaj. It was lurching along the route, so was its owner who did the same along the path of life.

The radio kept sending out a noisy sound. He didn't feel in the mood for listening to it; yet he didn't turn the device off once the sound of a singer was aired singing "Strutting past you, leaving you alone with your cruelty, I abandoned you forever." Listening to that single piece of music could stir up old memories of places and events. Shortly afterwards, he got into a muddle staggering from one thought to the next.

He switched the radio off once he heard the announcer's voice at the end of that piece of music. He looked at his watch; it was forty minutes past midnight. All of a sudden, several stains on the sleeve of his coat came into his notice. Unlike other stains on his reputation through life, these ones received his full attention. It didn't take time to learn they are stains of blood. He stuck out his tongue and began to lick them up. It changed his mood, as if he had fallen into a trance, as if he had been licking a woman's body. Suddenly, his mood swung, and his brain sent out a new signal. He spat his saliva out and then angrily wiped it off with his hand; after all, he didn't like spitting in his car. Having rolled the window down, he stuck his head out, notwithstanding the pouring rain, and started spitting on the road. During the interval between each round of spitting, he would turn his head to the sky to let the rain wash his mouth. He also stuck his hand out in order to have it cleaned up. Such a miserable condition did not stop him from putting his foot on the gas pedal. The jalopy was moving along, pulling to the right and to the left. He was in such terrible mood that he wasn't thinking about the cars coming from behind, nor was he careful about his own driving. He did not also pay any attention to the horn of another car trying to warn him. But he regained consciousness after a sharp rock burst his tire.

The car grounded to a halt. The headlights lit up the skirt of a hill with the wiper still on. Gazing into the space, he was looking at the veins of muddy water running down the hill. It seemed to remind him of his life, which had gotten stuck in the mud, unlikely to get out.

One hour later, he stopped by a café, standing alone with a feeble light pouring out. He had arrived with a burst tire and with the wheel on the left side sending out black smoke. It had heated up, so had his entire body; he felt a raging thirst in that rainy, cold night. Regardless of the time, he walked toward the café. He knocked at the closed door. Nobody answered, so he did it again. Nobody bothered to answer again. The next time, he knocked more loudly. This time, a young man appeared at the slightly open door. Hardly had the young man said that the café was closed before he pushed the door open and went in. He interrupted the young man when he wanted to object to his behavior.

"Bring me arak,[8]" he said.

The young man, who, for the day to come, had just put chairs and tables in order, was to join his wife waiting for him at the backroom under a warm blanket.

"Prices triple so late at night in such weather," said the young man, who had his mind blown by the request expressed by the midnight customer.

"I will pay you four times as much, just don't keep me waiting long," replied the customer.

---

[8]   A kind of alcoholic drink.

The young man guided the midnight customer to one of the tables and went to bring arak. The refrigerator was in the backroom, where his wife was awaiting him on a welcoming bed.

"I'm sleepy When the hell do you wrap it up?" asked his wife.

The young man, ready for the big hug of his wife, approached her and kissed her chubby face, which looked attractive to him.

"We've got a customer thirsty for arak," said the young man to his wife and went on to say, "Do you remember asking me for a two Kashan velvet blankets this evening?"

"With two male and female tigers on it," replied the wife.

"I will get them for you this week, but remember not to tell the boss we served a customer in the middle of the night," the young man told his wife.

It was still rainy out there, and the man who had just arrived with a decrepit Opel was now in good spirits inside the café. After talking about the Kashan velvet blanket, the young man wanted to lose no time in getting rid of the midnight customer and to be received instantly by his wife's warm hug. The customer, however, was a wet blanket. The drink seemed to have put him in an excellent mood. He forgot everything. He didn't think about the stains of blood nor about his dilapidated Opel with a burst tire. He no longer had any idea of where he was and why he was there.

"I will sleep here tonight," said the customer after staring at the young man's face.

It put the young man on edge, making him find a way to get rid of the customer. Meanwhile, the door swung open, and another man having a stylish raincoat on appeared at the door. He closed his umbrella, with water dropping from it, and made his way to the middle of the café.

"What do you want here?" the young man asked him, frustrated by the presence of the second customer, adding "The café is closed."

The second customer looked at the first one sitting at the table and made the young man understand that the café is not closed.

"I just need some eggs, I'm craving fried eggs," said the man.

"At this time, and in such weather, the price of egg changes," the young man, with the thought of Kashan velvet blanket, said mumbling.

"I don't mind," replied the second man.

The young man brought two dozen of eggs, and when the second customer was about to pay for them, he pointed at his first customer and asked the new customer, "This man wants to stay somewhere tonight. Can you give him the address of anywhere to stay?"

The second customer didn't reply; he took the eggs and left.

The young man, who felt completely at ease with the second customer, approached the first one and implored, "Man, I want to sleep. I have to wake up early in the morning."

"So do I. Do you mind if we sleep together?" replied the driver of the clapped-out Opel.

At the same time, the door was pushed open, and the man in the smart raincoat stood at the door. The stunned young man stared at him surprisingly, and the second customer directed his attention at the driver of the down-at-hill Opel.

"Who is he?" the second customer asked the young man.

He replied, "I have no idea sir. He has just drunk two bottles of arak. I suppose he is an easygoing man."

Half an hour later, a white *Aria*[9] pulled over in front of a villa standing by a river; the two customers of the *Siahbishe*[10] Café got out of the car while it was still raining.

"My name is Mohsen," said the man in the raincoat.

"My name is Kazem," said the driver of the tatty Opel.

Later on, both were sitting by the fireplace, with the smell of fried eggs and charred firewood filling the atmosphere around them.

A bottle of cognac was resting on the table, which was half empty. They both had turned their faces downward, staring at the floor; their attention, however, was focused on somewhere else. They felt something has hung around their necks, which made them feel short of breath. Then, some thoughts started to flash their gloomy minds, and their tongues began to get them across.

---

[9]   Rambler American, a passenger car, used to be sold under the name of Aria in Iran.

[10]   A village in Northern Iran.

"I was lucky to meet you at the café. Otherwise, I would have been overwhelmed with grief by morning," said Mohsen.

"You're entangled with a lady, aren't you?" asked Kazem as he was yawning.

"I tried my best to tame her, but I couldn't do so. She does whatever she likes. I have bought her a golden necklace yesterday, but she didn't appear tonight. I don't know where the hell she is."

"Women all behave the same. The more you run after them, the more they get elusive. The more you treat them well, the more harmful they get to you. They are devoid of kindness."

Kazem took another shot of cognac and asked, "Let me know. Is yours pretty?"

Mohsen replied after taking another shot, "I wish she weren't, but she was mine."

Kazem added, "Mine was pretty too. As long as she needed me, she would sleep with me in the garage. When she got my money, she called me stinky."

Suddenly, the light shed by fire made Kazem aware of some stains on his pants. He learned that they are stains of blood. All of a sudden, he got enraged, holding his pants between his fingers as if he was about to choke someone to death. He grabbed a knife, cut off those stains, and threw them into the fire. When his cut cloth caught fire, he burst into laughter. He enjoyed watching the scene. Mohsen had fallen asleep, not able to be aware of his guest's delight.

Mohsen was snoring, but Kazem was still awake. He kept saying "I'm parched." He rose to his feet, reeling to the kitchen. He was still thirsty and craving a glass of cold water. Reaching the kitchen, he turned the light on. There was a picture frame resting on a table; it held a woman's picture. He bowed over, blinking his eyes to get a clear view of it. When he managed to see the woman clearly, he gazed at it and said, "Damn! She springs to my mind at all times. She appears in front of my eyes, even in this picture."

When police opened the trunk of the broken down Opel the morning after, they came across the bloody body of the woman whose picture was sitting on the table in Mohsen's kitchen.

From then on, whenever the young waiter of Siahbishe slept with his wife under the Kashan velvet blanket, the thought of the two midnight customers crossed his mind.

The Laughing Humpback

NEARLY ALL THE people living in the town were well familiar with Abbas Ghouzi.[11] He used to carry Haj[12] Sadegh's rolls of fabric on his back, delivering them to the customers across Tehran's neighborhoods.

He was one-meter tall, but due to a hump rising from his right shoulder, which made him stoop down, he seemed to be shorter. The twenty-three-year-old man had tolerable features. His posture when he was carrying several rolls of fabric made no difference from the time he was not carrying anything. He laughed frequently with his saliva spitting out; he wiped it out with his cuffs.

---

[11] Abbas the Humpback.

[12] A title given to someone who has made a pilgrimage to Mecca.

Haj Sadegh was a family man, possessing a big house in Sangelaj.[13] He let out a room across the yard to Abbas Ghousi and his sister, Zahra, who was three years his junior. Zahra used to serve Haj Sadegh and his family as a waitress. She swept the yard, washed clothes, and helped Haj Sadegh's wife with shopping. Haj Sadegh used to fool around with her behind his wife's back. Zahra and his brother, Abbas, had lost their mother two years ago. Haj Sadegh had taken them in not out of humanity but to enjoy Zahra's body and to drudge Abbas.

Haj Sadegh had three shops in Bazaar-e Bazzazha,[14] selling all kinds of cloth, woolen textiles, chintz, chelvar,[15] muslin, canvas, calico, cotton, voile, shawl, broadcloth, and women's clothing. He treated his customers with a friendly manner, asking them in and inviting them for a glass of tea. The customers, however, knew how sly he was, and even if they had bought something at one – third of the price, they had no doubt he had taken them in.

Bazaar-e-Bazzazha had become famous for slyness, yet it made no sense to Abbass Ghouzi. He might have been unaware of what was going around. He just laughed and took order from Haj Sadegh. He used to put some rolls of fabric on his back, carrying them to Oudlajan.[16]

---

[13] A neighborhood in southern Tehran.

[14] A shopping center for supplying and selling fabrics.

[15] A tightly woven white cotton fabric.

[16] An old neighborhood in Southern Tehran.

At night, when he had dinner and went to sleep across the room away from his sister, he remained silent and gazed at the ceiling.

Out of sympathy, one had recited the story of "A Hunch over the Hunch". Once upon a time, a hunchback went to a hammam[17] early in the morning. The binehdar[18] wished him a good omen as the first customer of the hammam. The man entered the bath, seeing a group who were clapping and dancing. He assumed a groom had been taken to the public bath, joining them in clapping and dancing. Finally, a member of that crowd came to him and offered a massage to relieve him of tiredness. When the massage came to an end, the man got rid of his hunch. It came out to be the wedding of a genie.[19]

From then on, he circulated the story across the town. When another hunchback heard the story, he decided to go to the hammam untimely to ask the genies for disposing him of his hunch. When he reached the hammam, however, it was their morning ceremony. Unaware of the event, he started to dance. Therefore, genies got outraged, putting another hunch on his shoulder.

---

[17] A traditional public bath.

[18] The cashier of the hammam.

[19] A magical creature in old Arabian stories that will do what you want when you call it (Longman Dictionary of Contemporary English, fourth edition).

Abbas kept laughing at the story whenever it flashed through his head, falling asleep every night with the thought of it crossing his mind.

One day, when Abbas was sitting by the hauz[20] washing his face and hands, Haj Sadegh appeared from the vestibule[21] and asked him to stay at the shop after he opened its doors. Abbas agreed and left. Haj Saddegh was going to send his wife to Emam Zadeh Davood.[22] Haj Khanum[23] had the intention of staying there for a week in order to pray day and night, to which Haj Sadegh agreed upon; it would give him the opportunity for staying alone with Zahra. He had just one concern that kept bothering him: his eighteen-year-old daughter, Forugh. Haj Khanum had ordered Zahra to watch Forugh during her husband's and her absence. She was the family's only child, with a boy losing his life to typhoid at sixteen and another girl dying at birth.

After Haj Khanum had left home for the Emam Zadeh, Haj Sadegh began to flirt with Zahra. He would

---

[20] A large pool used to be designed and built in Iranian traditional houses.

[21] A vestibule [vɛstɪbjuːl] is a lobby, entrance hall, or passage between the entrance and the interior of a building (Wikipedia).

[22] A sacred place near Tehran, which is the tomb of a descendant of the prophet, where people visit to make a pilgrimage.

[23] A title for the women who had the experience of visiting Mecca.

leave home late in the morning and leave his shop early in the afternoon. During his absence, he ordered Abbas to keep his eyes glued to the fabrics.

One morning, Forugh told her father that she wanted to take a bath in the public hammam in the company of Zahra. He said that Zahra must stay at home to prepare dinner for his guests, asking Abbas to carry the stuff used for bathing and wait for Forugh outside the hammam to accompany her home.

"When do you go to the Bazaar?" asked Abbas.

Haj Sadegh replied, "I told you I have guests, didn't I? Today, it is off."

Putting the stuff Forugh wanted to use for bathing over his back, he followed Forugh after she left home. Haj Sadegh too licked his chops and walked to Zahra's room across the yard. Hardly had she tidied up the room when Sadegh appeared at the entrance.

Meanwhile, Forugh was walking through the maze of narrow streets with Abbas following her. He had never walked so close to her; if so, he had failed to pay a careful attention. He had just watched Forugh from a long distance. Now he focused his full attention on her, with her buttocks moving up and down under her flower-dotted chador. Little by little, he began to get the picture of what was going on. The scene had his mouth watered as if there was a jar of honey standing in front of him. He was unintentionally pushing the hammam stuff against his body.

Reaching the hammam, Forugh turned to take the stuff. For the first time, Abbas saw the face of Forugh so clearly, with black doe eyes and two long, curved eyebrows. He had pursed lips and made a sharp glance.

"I will wait here by the time you come back," said Abbas as Haj Sadegh had ordered him.

Forugh pulled the curtain and entered the hammam, leaving Abbas alone with his heart pounding. He unintentionally sat on a step leading to the hammam, so a pedestrian protested his behavior. For the first time, he let laughter go and looked daggers at the passerby. He was forced to sit on the ground further ahead. At the same time, a flock of pigeons flying overhead drew his attention; he started to laugh again. Pigeons flew away, but Abbas was still looking overhead. He weighed a thought crossing his mind. Then he stood up, curiously looking around. After waiting for a short time, he approached a tree twenty meters ahead; when he learned nobody was walking along the street, he climbed the tree like a lizard, and then he jumped on a wall. He crawled over the attached roofs and reached the hammam's roof.

There were some windows on hammam's roof, designed in such a way that the sunlight could enter the interior space of the hammam and light it up. Abbas checked all the windows one by one to find Forugh. He saw women's naked bodies, but he was just looking for Forugh. Finally, he found her under one of the showers. Forugh had soaped herself and was washing her body under the shower. Abbas's eyes stopped roving as he saw Forugh. He was like a hungry person watching the food over the window. Abbas was disarticulated, but his whole body cried instead of him: "I wish I were the comb to your hair. I wish I were the towel around your waist. I wish I were the sponge rolling over your flower-like body."

Unaware of Abbas's curious look, Forugh was rubbing her hands over her head and neck with a flirtatious coquetry typical of newly matured girl. She pushed her hands against her chest, toying with her belly and the area surrounding it. Abbas Ghouzi was on the roof, roaming the heaven. Though speechless, he was now aware that some other things did also matter other than putting fabrics on his shoulder.

At the same time, when he was still watching the scene, the call for prayer rose from a neighboring roof. It was noon, the time that people were supposed to pray. Muazzen turned his face to let his voice circulate around. Suddenly, he saw Abbas and shouted at him, "You motherfucker, shame on you!"

Abbas fled immediately and climbed down the tree, waiting for Forugh to leave the hammam. Now he didn't bother to stop cracking up. He kept giggling and pondering.

"I don't like them, they are always denying my rights."

When his mother was alive, he used to stealthily watch her during the praying. She called upon Imams to guarantee her son's well-being while touching the prayer beads. Once, he saw his mother looking heavenward, telling God, "Now that you have denied my son's rights and gave him to me with a hunch on his back, at least secure his happiness."

Abbas's head was still facing downward while waiting for Forugh. He was after his rights and was thinking of Forugh's body. He didn't know her body had already aroused someone's interest, and a woman had chosen Forugh as her would-be daughter-in-law. He was also unaware that Haj Sadegh had deceived Abbas's sister into losing her virginity.

Poor Zahra had got used to Haj Sadegh's insipid pranks. She disliked him, and at the same time, she felt beholden to him, but she was unaware how dirty-natured he was.

When Forugh's mother came back home from Emam Zadeh Davood, the family of the boy whose mother saw Forugh at the hammam asked for her hand in marriage.

The marriage was scheduled for the end of Muharram and Safar. Haj Sadegh made everything ready for the event and prepared a large dowry for his daughter. But another mourning was awaiting Haj Sadegh's family after the Ashura's mourning ceremonies. It came to postpone the marriage forever.

One day, Forugh went mean to the basement for a hair removal. Please check.

She suddenly saw Abbas busy carrying the cartons of syrups and lemon juices.

Abbas Ghouzi got embarrassed and greeted her. Forugh didn't answer his greeting and asked him to get out of the basement.

"I'm doing the work of your wedding," said Abbas with bitter laughter.

"You, asshole, don't need to talk about it," retorted Forugh.

"Why? Aren't you happy?"

"It has nothing to do with you, get out of here you ugly hunchback."

Abbas sprang out like a scarred tiger and shut the basement door.

Two hours later, everybody was looking for Abbas and Forugh. Haj Sadegh called Abbas's name, and Haj Khanum called Forugh's name. When Zahra opened the basement door, she shouted out of horror, and silence dominated.

Forugh was lying on the floor bleeding, gagged by a cloth Abbas had put over her mouth. Abbas Ghouzi was in the corner and on the ground. With his dying breath, he said quietly, "At last, I got my rights."

A Love as Hot as
the Summer Heat

THE TRAIN ARRIVED in Ahvaz after blowing its whistle three times. It was a sweltering summer day, with autumn still a month away. As soon as Musayyeb got off the train, his face began to feel the merciless heat of summer. He took a look at his watch and rushed to the street. It was fifty minutes past noon. Passengers, and the people who were there to see them off or receive them, dotted the station. Musayyeb got to the street with beads of sweat appearing on his forehead. He wiped them off and jumped at the first taxi appearing at his sight. He sat next to the driver and put his only bag in front of him. He ordered the driver to get him straight to his destination.

The taxi stopped across Arabnia Street, and Musayyeb got out. He looked at the street curiously and began to walk along. The street was not bustling with many people, and nothing was heard except for the noise of air conditioners. The heat of the day had forced everybody to stay at home.

Musayyeb faced an elderly man who was limping with a stick. He greeted the old man, who was gasping for breath, and walked past him. A few steps ahead, he saw two young women veiled from head to toe walking toward him. He turned his face down and strode past them. The two women were busy speaking and giggling. Having seen Musayyeb, they covered their face with their veils and got silent. Musayyeb, however, paid no attention to them, just thinking deeply about Esmat. He had fallen in love with Esmat a year ago when he was on the roof during pigeon racing. All of a sudden, Esmat and her chubby thighs caught his attention. From then on, he would stay on the roof, watching Esmat stealthily. Three weeks into it, his mother caught him off guard. She got outraged and tore him to shreds, as if Esmat was her daughter and Musayyeb was a stranger who had been looking daggers at her.

"Don't get me wrong," said Musayyeb to his mother. "I didn't know how to tell you to ask her hand in marriage.

His mother felt at ease as if the excuse had relieved her of his sin, but she told him, with a feeling of regret and rebuke, "How? At twenty, you're involved in pigeon racing. You have never studied nor do you work. Then you expect Haji Ghanbar to let you marry his daughter!"

Musayyeb fell silent. Never did he go to the roof again out of his mother's fear. He hung on in the hope that one day he would come face-to-face with Esmat on the street. Haji Ghanbar, though, was not the kind of man to let his daughter leave the house alone. One week went by. Musayyeb's aunt got home from a one-month trip to Mashhad. His aunt adored Musayyeb, who was the sole reminder of his late brother, and so did Musayyeb to his aunt. He used to have a great time at her house, which was located at the end of the same street. The not-too-talkative aunt, a sixty-three-year-old woman with white hair, had sharp eyes and was in full possession of all her faculties. It enabled her to notice a change in Musayyeb's behavior.

"You have changed a lot over the last month that I was not here," she said.

"Nothing important has happened," replied Musayyeb, claiming he was looking for a job.

"Speak your mind," she told him and added, "Looking for a job doesn't drive anyone to despair."

"Leave me alone," said Musayyeb.

"Tell me the truth, do you," she asked.

"No, my dear," said Musayyeb.

His aunt went on, "Don't lie to me. Let me know who she is. I will do what I can. Your happiness makes my late brother happy too."

It lightened his loads such as a bird that is released from the cage. He was encouraged into confessing how much he loved Esmat.

The aunt got stunned for she was well familiar with Haji Ghanbar. She knew how much he was entangled with money and his family's honor, and gaining his satisfaction, in this respect, is a pain in the neck. She asked Musayyeb to face the fact. Musayyeb, regardless of what she said, was blind with love and turned a deaf ear to her advice; otherwise, he would have put it out of his mind the first day his mother called upon him to do so. He couldn't do so, and he was after a way to get to Esmat.

"If someone let Esmat in on it and she might like you too, there might be a change in the situation," added the aunt after she found Musayyeb so determined.

Musayyeb asked, "How is it possible? They don't even let her get out of the house."

She replied, "They are right to do so. After all, she is their daughter."

"I'm just waiting to meet her after schools reopen," said Musayyeb.

"You don't need to be anxious," replied his aunt.

One day three weeks later, the aunt told Musayyeb, "Esmat has come to love you too."

It made his day, and he asked with enthusiasm, "How? Aunt, you're the best!"

"You must pass on your best wishes to Akhtar Bandandaz," she replied.

"Why? You have made your mark."

"Don't get on the wrong track. It was her silver tongue that made her do a good job of it. Otherwise, I would not be able to do anything. I got her to show your photo to Esmat, then she began to speak well of you. Last but not least, she talked her into feeling like seeing you."

Musayyeb was raring to go, asking, "When? Where? How?"

One week later, Esmat left home for rouzeh[24] in the company of her mother and some other women. Regardless of the others, she fell behind others to see Musayyeb's face as he was standing on a street corner.

When they got face-to-face, excitement pulsed through their hearts. They wished all the people around would disappear at that moment so that they would remain alone. They wished time would stop, and they would look at one another from then on. But they lost hopes when her mother's voice was raised, calling on her to hurry up.

Now, they were both involved in a growing bilateral love. One day, Musayyeb's mother went to the bath; he took the opportunity and stealthily approached the roof to take a look at Esmat. After he laid secretly in the sun for about an hour, Esmat appeared again in the yard. Musayyeb threw a pebble at her. Feeling embarrassed, she hid behind a date palm to prevent Musayyeb from seeing her uncovered hair. She secretly looked at him and smiled. Musayyeb pointed his finger at the roof and asked her to come to the roof. She first feared but couldn't resist the temptation and climbed the stairs leading to the roof a few minutes later. He approached her with his back folded. First, they were speechless for a minute. They gazed at each other, and for a while, they stared downward. Their hearts were beating strongly. Esmat let her chador move back, and again, she pulled it ahead.

---

[24] A religious gathering at which the tragedy of Karbalah is recalled.

"I like to see you every day, what about you?" said Musayyeb.

"I'm fearful," she said.

"Of me?" he asked.

"Not of you," she replied.

At that very moment, Esmat's mother called her.

"Where are you, Esmat? I'm busy. Turn the stove down."

Esmat left immediately, throwing Musayyeb into turmoil.

From then on, they would meet each other secretly on the roof. Their date was dominated with fear and apprehension. One day, Esmat gave a piece of disappointing news to Musayyeb.

"Someone has asked me for my hand in marriage," she said.

It gave Musayyeb a fright and asked unintentionally, "Did you agree?"

"I'm not the person who must agree to it," she replied.

"Have you ever seen him? Who is he? Do you love him?"

"I do love you."

"So you shouldn't marry him."

"They will kill me. Akhtar Khanum said It's a shame Musayyeb does not have a job'."

Musayyeb felt he would like to melt into the ground. It was the first time that a feeling of frivolity swept over him. Now he came to know that the father's name and fame is not a matter of importance. It is a person's nature that matters. When Akhtar Bandandaz felt pity for him, he must have been in hot water. He turned around twice and said, "I left my pigeon from the very first time I saw you. You have grabbed my attention. Today I will travel to Shiraz to start a job. Someone has offered me a job, but I have yet to agree to it. But I will go now. I will go and return with money to persuade Haji Ghanbar into letting me marrying you."

Musayyeb left Esmat alone. Haji Ghanbar was in a hurry to get his daughter wedded. Esmat's tears did not dissuade her father out of it. His aunt's plans carried out through Akhtar Bandandaz were dead in the water too.

Three months later, Esmat was forced into getting married. At the wedding night, all the guests saw a groom forty years older than the bride. Nobody dared to say anything. All the people were speechless as if they were watching a herd of sheep being sent to the slaughterhouse. In the nuptial chamber, the groom, who was experiencing his third wife, stripped Esmat's clothes off and jumped at her like an old hyena. A feeling of nausea came over her by his pungent smell. She closed her eyes and sought Musayyeb in her mind. Sometimes she felt it was Musayyeb who was toying with her naked body.

Six months later, her parents were killed in a car crash on the way to Qom. They were on a pilgrimage. A thought struck her after she heard the news. Every time she got laid with the old hyena, she cursed her parents.

Now she was free and in constant contact with Akhtar Bandandaz. She kept inquiring about Musayyeb. The aunt reminded her of a sin she was committing for Esmat was married. At last, her trick bore fruit, and Akhtar managed to gain Musayyeb's address through his aunt. She gave the address to Esmat.

When she took the address, she felt as if Musayyeb was in her grip. She kept kissing it and thanking God. After she began to feel at ease, she wrote a letter and asked Musayyeb to ring the doorbell on 342 Arabnia Street at two o'clock in the afternoon on Tuesday, on the thirtieth day of Mordad.[25]

Musayyeb was still marching along Arabnia Street, and these thoughts kept crossing his mind. When the two young veiled women walked past Musayyeb with *sangak* bread in their hands, he took a looked at his watch. It was five minutes to two in the afternoon. Then he kept looking at the numbers. By the time he reached 342, he could easily hear his heart beating. It was going to jump out of his chest. He closed his eyes for a while to think carefully of the thought crossing his mind. He opened his eyes. Hardly had he rung the bell before the door opened and Esmat's smiling face appeared before him.

Musayyeb just managed to say Esmat. But she was all over him. Musayyeb had been waiting for this moment for months. He was embracing the woman he was in love with, but since he knew Esmat did not belong to him, he stepped back. He wanted to find out about the nature of the help she had asked for in her letter.

Esmat wasted no time and said, "Everything has come to an end. We are travelling to Kuwait."

"What are you talking about? What about your husband?"

---

[25] The fifth month of the Iranian calendar.

"I don't have a husband anymore. Now it is me, you, and my suitcase."

Esmat put her chador on, stepped out of the house, and closed the door.

Musayyeb was unaware of her plan, so he asked, "Shouldn't I know what is going on?"

She replied, "Hurry up. We should rush to the lanj. Nakhoda[26] Housein is waiting for us. I will tell you the story on the lanj."

A few minutes later, they disappeared at the end of Arabnia Street.

On Thursday, a news report appeared on newspapers. It read, "An elderly man's body was found at 342 Arabnia Street. He has died of poisoning, and his wife is unaccounted for."

---

[26] A title for sailors.

Thirsty on the Ocean

THAT DAY, THE young fisherman woke up earlier than usual. He sat on the edge of his bed and unintentionally gazed out at the sea.

His compact parental house lay on the skirt of a hill facing the sea. It was just one of the decrepit row houses sprawling the hill. Most wives were busy selling fish and vegetables at the island's sole market. Their men went to sea for fishing. One night, his father left home to sail across the sea to catch large fishes; from then on, he had never got ashore anymore. He left his wife and the young fisherman alone. His mother used to sell fish, fruits, and vegetables at the market. He also used to go to sea to catch fish when he had been caught by a mermaid himself. She managed to make him jittery and jumpy.

He was about to spread his net across the water when he heard a noise not far behind. He suddenly saw a young girl swimming toward him. She complained of tiredness and called on him to let her rest on the boat. He forgot about the net and held her hands. It made him flare up—her attractive body with a pair of bikini on fanned the flame of his passion. Never had he faced such a tempting girl on the island. Her skin was tanned, with the sunlight having left it in a rich color. Her wet blond hair, from which drops of water were falling down, was in sharp contrast with her blue eyes, just like the young fisherman's heart battling that of the swimmer girl. The girl was also lusting after him—with his curly hair, tanned face, and well-built chest—stirring excitement inside her. His kind, curious look aroused her passion too.

They were both alone across the seas. The looks and strange silence worked well to bring them together. They found themselves united. They were thirsty in the middle of a large body of water. Now it was time for the girl who had caught the fisherman to bid farewell. He asked her where she was residing. She pointed at a small white ship anchored a few miles ahead.

The girl left, and the fisherman's net remained empty. The thought of her made him unconscious. As the darkness fell, he gazed at the sea out of the window to see the white ship. He just saw the flashes of light emitted from the windows and other parts of the ship in the gloom. Peering over the window, he asked himself, "Which beam of light is touching my mermaid's face?" At last, he dropped off to sleep out of exhaustion. Early in the morning, he woke up sitting on the edge of his bed, but when he looked at the sea, the ship was not in sight anymore. The mermaid had swum off.

Wounded Snake

THEY WERE BOTH above fifty. One of them had a whitish thick beard. His hair was grizzled, but his eyebrows had yet to turn white. His features were oldish, but his well-developed, stout body suggested he was a strong man. The other man, who was sitting in front of him and smoking a pipe, had a kepi cap on. He was tall and lean with a shaved face. They were both sitting at the table of a café located on the corner of the city square. Two cups of coffee were on the table.

The man with the kepi cap gave several dry coughs and said, "I've got no doubt that this disease will bump me off."

"How do you know?"

"When your days are numbered, you would feel it. My only concern is my daughter, who loves your son, as you know. If she marries him, I will feel at ease. I will then think nothing of death."

The boy's father took a sip of his coffee and said, "Hearing this remark is surprising. When I was in dire straits, it was you that gave me hope."

The girl's father took a deep puff at his pipe and replied, "Nobody can fight against sunset, even Elpis."

The boy's father folded his hands and went on, "You need a journey."

"I'm already on the journey."

"Not these kinds of trips. If I weren't on the shift today, I'd take you to a short trip which could pave a new way before you. We would pay a visit to the grandmother. She is still a lively, loving, and kind lady. She still feels like living." Then, he looked his watch and added, "Two hours later, I must guide the eastward train toward the west. If I had enough cash, I would get someone else to run the train to enjoy your company."

"You are a good friend. I feel beholden to you. Now you should go on your duty."

"As soon as I am off, I will visit you."

The train snaked its way out of the tunnel from an urban station, speeding up on the twisting railway. The son's father was monitoring the route and the gauges when a young woman hurriedly rushed into the control cabin. She was watching around to be certain nobody had chased her. The girl, who was holding a bag, told the father, "Don't panic. I'm not here to bother you. I just need your help."

He got unruffled and told the frightened cute girl, "You must not be here. It's too dangerous, especially today, when an isolated car is completely under control by the police forces. You'd better get out of here before long."

On the verge of tears, the girl pleaded, "I've got a good reason to be here. I put myself at risk to get to you."

She then took out a wad of bills and added, "A part of it is yours, and I swear I'll bring you further money. I'm from a wealthy family. I'll give you anything you will. You just need to find an excuse and stop two kilometers off the second station, where I am able to free my prisoner. I don't know why I'm here and saying these things to you. I just begged you to stop there. Some folks are there to help us cross the border."

After a look at the wads of bills, it occurred to him that they could change his life. They could pave the way for a high life for his son and his friend's daughter. He resisted the temptation though and replied, "Dear gal! You'd better get out of here before you get into trouble too. I have always led an honorable life, and never do I destroy the remaining part of my life."

She knelt down and tearfully pleaded. The man, who didn't want to stain his reputation, was standing like a stony statue with closed eyes. He just recalled the warning issued by the police that ordered him to blow the whistle three times in case of facing suspected cases. He did so while the girl was ignorant of what was going to happen. One of the four police forces, who were watching a prisoner, rushed to the cabin and arrested her. The outrageous girl turned to the man, spit on him, and shouted, "Filthy animal! You support a law whose agent has raped me and jailed my friend who has supported me. Shame on you, asshole!"

The police pushed the girl forward, and the son's father shockingly spread out on the seat.

The train, like a venomous snake that wants to clear everything on its way, wound its way along until it reached the destination. Police took the prisoner out to transfer him to a notorious jail. The son's father gazed at him over the window of his cabin. The boy was chained up by his feet and hands, and the girl was handcuffed too. When they walked closer, they became more and more visible; all of a sudden, the man collapsed and coiled like a wounded snake. The prisoner was his son, whom he assumed had been on a trip.

The Uncle

W HEN HE LEARNED the Uncle was sick and had left for the house located in the middle of their garden in the north, he invoked the destiny of the Inuit. When an Inuit learns it is his turn to pass away, he suddenly disappears. They travel far afield, so that their body is buried under the ice and snow of the North Pole. They were well in accord, the age difference notwithstanding. When Arash felt gloomy, he didn't hesitate to visit the Uncle. The Uncle would listen to him patiently and then calm him down with some pleasant remarks. Now it was the Uncle's turn, and it was upon Arash to pacify him.

When Arash was at the wheel, negotiating the twisting curves of the road leading to the north, his hand seemed to be leafing through his memoir at the same time. On any leaf was a shadow of the Uncle. It reminded him of his first love and the helps offered by the Uncle leading to his marriage to Jaleh.

A broad smile spread over his face when he looked back to his premarriage memories and the time he was a teenager. It empowered him a lot. He recalled the first glass of arak, which the Uncle offered him. He stood behind him and said, "Drink heartily, my dear! But don't let it captivate you. If so, it will burn you to ashes."

He looked back to the day when he wrote a bad check. When he found himself in hot water, his father started to shout at him. Meanwhile, the Uncle mediated and said, "Why do you lash out at him? Let him experience it! Don't you want to make a man out of him?"

As soon as Arash left the Kandovan tunnel, light sprinkle clouded his vision. As he switched on the wiper, the beauties of the north caught his eyes. The weather was gorgeous. The light drops of rain were refreshing the road, mountain, trees, and grasslands. Arash played a piece of pop song recorded on a tape the Uncle recommended he buy. The singer, Gita, sang, "If it is love, if it is life, I don't let my eyes see the world."

His eyes became watery, and tears began to stream down his face after a while. He pressed the gas pedal to the floor to join the Uncle sooner. Arriving at the garden, he found the door ajar. As usual, the Uncle had left the door open as a sign of hospitality. Arash just needed to open the gate as much as there was enough space for his car to be pulled in, directing his car to an old house standing in the middle of the garden. He stopped at the door and rushed into the building.

The Uncle had been snoozing on a leather armchair by the fireplace whose fire was going out. Next to him were some bottles of pill and a cough syrup on a table.

The Uncle opened his eyes as though he could recognize Arash from his smell. He broke into a wide smile and said, "I was sure you'd come." He added, "If only all the people were friends with one another."

"Uncle! They have told me you are ill. You have been obstinate. You left home and came here on your own. Half an hour after my arrival from Shiraz, I set off."

The Uncle replied, "It was kind of you to come here, but my illness is nonsense. As it is clear, I'm as tough as a bear." As he pushed away his blanket and rose to his feet, he said, "I've been waiting for you to drink a glass and have a heart-to-heart talk. Nobody is immortal anyway."

The Rose Offered
by the Beloved

HE SEEMED TO have left no stone unturned on the lookout for a prey in the forest in the past three days. He knew by experience, and others had told him, where deer usually appear. But three days passed with no trace of them by day or night. He ascended huge rocks with the help of his gun several times, only to spot no deer on the mountainside.

Halfway up the mountain, he spotted a rolling cloud of smoke rising toward the sky. He had assumed that nobody other than him was in the forest.

An hour later, he reached a cottage in the middle of the forest, whose chimney was blowing out smoke. It was cold, but he was hot, dripping with beads of sweat. His search for something to hunt and combing the wood for deer had taken the chill off. The heat inside the wooden building really mattered to him. It was the fourth day since he said good-bye to the coziness of his home. He couldn't resist the temptation to knock on the door. He felt like putting off his boots to let his feet get refreshed, taking off his sheepskin coat and lying supine on the ground. He wanted to satisfy a craving for a sip of hot tea. Suddenly, a kind, strong voice interrupted his thought, "I enjoy receiving guests in here as God has likened them to his friends."

His dream came true, lying supine with his bare feet respiring. Steam was rising from a glass of hot tea next to him.

Again, he heard the deep voice of the host. He said, "Sometimes the forest animals disappear, and nobody knows where they go and why they have gone."

The guest, who was enjoying his well-earned rest, did not reply and glued his eyes to the ceiling.

The host, who was trying to hide his smile spreading across his face, went on to say, "What are you doing in the forest? Hunting might have been an excuse, isn't it?"

The guest replied, "You're right. A girl has charmed me. Her father is tough on me. He keeps testing me in different ways. This time, he asked me for restless prey."

"A few miles away, there is a pond by which some deer have been spotted occasionally," the host said. "But I advise you against sleeping by it for everyone who has done so has been hallucinated."

He made it to the pond, and unluckily, there was no deer by it. Feeling tired, he put down his gun, rested against a tree, and fell asleep under a slightly overcast sky. He dreamed that his beloved, who had endeared herself to him, was approaching him. She hugged him, offering a fresh red rose to him. They shagged over the grassland, giving each other passionate kisses. Their moans of pleasure scared the birds away.

All of a sudden, he woke to the rumble of a thunder. He fearfully looked around, but his beloved was out of sight. The first drops of rain started to fall, getting his face wet. To dry it up, he thrust his hand into his pocket to take out a handkerchief. He did so, only to see the rose his beloved had given to him slip out.

Solmaz and Saghakhaneh's[27] Candles

THE SKY WAS overcast. It was not raining though. The door had swung open slightly, and Solmaz was peering through the narrow space at her mother who was hanging her husband's shirt on the washing line.

Solmaz was sitting next to an oil-burning stove on which there was a pot of boiling water. She was peeling potatoes. When she saw how her mother was taking pains to hang her father's adorned shirt on the washing line. She wished one day she would do so with Sohrab's shirts.

Solmaz had yet to lose her virginity and was waiting for someone to ask for her hand in marriage. Solmaz had a crush on Sohrab, a young man with a muscular chest who used to go to the forest in the company of her father to collect wood. Her father adorned Sohrab as much as his shirt. Solmaz used to watch the comings and goings of Sohrab carefully as much as her mother used to take care of her father's shirt. Whenever she offered him a cup of tea at the order of her father, a faint smile crept over her face. Meanwhile, Sohrab's heart began to pound in his chest, and he felt like taking her in his arms.

Sohrab had learned what Solmaz was trying to say with all those smiles and looks, but he did not dare to disclose his own feelings or to say anything beyond usual greetings out of fear of her father. He was well aware that the respond to any immature behavior would be an overreaction on the part of her father, who could cut a log in half with his sharp, heavy ax.

From the time Solmaz hit it off with Sohrab, she would visit their neighborhood's saghakhaneh located in the middle of the forest. She would ask her mother to accompany her to prevent her father from lashing out at her for going out on her own. Her mother would watch her lighting candles and mumbling to herself. Then they would return home with the daughter having a lump in her throat.

Solmaz kept masking her feelings, and every time her mother asked Solmaz to tell her the truth, she would say she was praying for the health of her parents. Finally, her mother, who had once experienced flame of desire, caught on to the fact after she noticed her smile at Sohrab while offering a cup of tea to him.

One day, on the way home from the saghakhaneh with the candles still on, she said, "We're women. We cannot hide our feelings from one another. I will talk to your father tonight."

Her eyes lighted up with excitement, and tears of joy streamed down her cheeks.

When her parents went to bed at night, her father said, "I'm so happy tonight."

Her mother replied, "You should as well make Solmaz happy."

Solmaz was eavesdropping, shivering with fear. She was waiting for her father's reaction.

But, when her mother let her father in on it, he sighed deeply and said, "I wish you had told me sooner. There is no one better than Sohrab."

A feeling of bliss came over her. But when her father said Sohrab was supposed to marry his cousin early next month, her face fell, and she looked crestfallen. Candles, which she had burned, flickered and went out too.

On the Cobbles of Paris

H E IS SUFFERING from persistent coughs. He keeps tossing and turning. He rises on his elbows several times and takes several sips of water.

It is cold and stormy out there. It is pouring, and drops of rain are striking the window.

Ahmed has slipped under the covers with a pair of jeans and a jacket on, but he is still shivering with cold. He regretfully takes a frequent look at the broken heater and then drops his gaze. The rent and the electricity are three-and-a-half months in arrears. He is in a bad way, and his emotionally divorced wife, now his roommate, is busy selling her body. Paris, which is nicknamed City of Love, is no doubt rich in young chicks, so there is no room for a displaced woman her age to show off; after all, she is now in her early forties, has gone into labor twice, and her homesickness has left her an emotional wreck.

Six months after she split up with her first husband, she married Ahmed and gave the children to her ex.

The occasional coughs have overwhelmed Ahmed. He has trouble breathing. He rises and shuffles across the room to the window. He assumes standing may ease respiration. But he says, "Breathing! I see breathing as death! To me, death is living!"

He spits on the wooden floor unintentionally. There is an old double bed, a decrepit wooden table and chair, an empty fridge, and a rusty stove, which is often cold. There is an old small radio on the table, which is off.

He is suffering from lingering coughs. He walks around the room and then looks over the window.

They have a room in an old flat in downtown Paris. Ahmed sees the upper part of the Eifel Tower. Lightning lights up the sky. Then, the roar of thunder is heard overhead. Thunder and lightning continue to rage.

Ahmed looks down. Cobbles are awash and reflecting the light. Meanwhile, a car is rolling forward. Ahmed gazes at it. His heart begins to beat in his chest. Coughs on one hand and his beating heart on the other are likely to bring him to his knees. The car pulls in. He is curious to know who is going to get out of it. His yesterday's wife and today's roommate leaves the car.

Ahmed walks away from the window and sits at the table. He is not able to stand or move anymore. He lowers his head and put it on his arms for a short time. He raises his head again and looks at the radio. He turns it on. "The voice of homeland," the radio announced.

Ahmed, who has not been able to move easily, roars like a lion, hitting the radio over at a stroke of his hand. It is muffled. The action gives him satisfaction, as if he was satisfied with a wonderful dish. It is momentary though. He hears a knock at the door. It is surprising. He assumes his wife has left her keys at the house. Unwillingly, he heads toward the door. Opening the door, he faces the landlord. He is short and stout, with a nightcap on. He is speaking French. His expression betrays his annoyance.

Ahmed says in French that he will settle his debt tomorrow.

The asshole leaves him alone, and he goes toward the blanket. Now the deadline set by the landlord adds insult to injury. At the same time, Fereshteh arrives. She has bought cough syrup, milk, cheese, honey, and bread. She put them on the table and put off her wet raincoat, throwing it on the chair. She asks how he is doing and sits.

"Are you still coughing?" she asks.

"I'm still breathing," he replied.

"I've got a cough syrup. It will undoubtedly soothe you," she said.

Fereshteh takes it out of its box and goes toward Ahmed.

Ahmed stares at her. She is still nice and lean. She does not seem like a person who is after a customer. He notices her torn skirt and asks, "What happened?"

She put the syrup on the table and walks toward the window indifferently.

"It got caught under his foot, and he didn't let me put it off."

Again, he is overwhelmed by his coughs and his heart rate.

Fereshteh gets worried and heads for him. She forces him to drink the syrup and says, "A man shouldn't turn his wife's request down."

"The roommate, not the wife," he shouts.

She puts the bottle on the table and goes toward her bed. She gets in unchanged and slips under the covers. She says before falling asleep, "I'm forced. And you haven't said anything."

Ahmed is silent. Perhaps the coughs may not let him talk.

"If it were against your will, you wouldn't do so," he replies a few seconds after the coughs have gone dead.

Fereshteh is asleep, so she doesn't hear his response. She has run out of steam and drifts off.

Next morning, Fereshteh wakes to a knock at the door. She faces the landlord after she has opened the door. Fereshteh goes to wake up Ahmed, but he is not on the bed. She looks at the window unintentionally, walking hesitantly toward it. Reaching the window, she looks down.

Ahmed's lifeless body is on the cobbles, and a few people are around it.

The sky is clear, and it is not raining anymore. But the cobbles before the old multistory building in downtown Paris are bloody and require cleaning.

Deep under the Waters of Chao Phraya[28]

---

[28] A major river in Thailand flowing through Bangkok.

MORTEZA HAD NOT shown his face at the UN for a few days. Whenever refugees visited there, Morteza was in evidence with his firsthand jokes to relieve their tensions over uncertainty.

The UN received refugees every day from nine in the morning to four in the afternoon, excluding Saturdays and Sundays.

That year, 2005, roughly two hundred people had made it to Thailand to seek asylum. Some Iranians were granted asylum, just waiting for the UN to inform them on the country they would be sent. Others, whose claims were in the maze of regulations, had a sense of foreboding. They were also worried about their cost of living. What would they do if they were out of money? Therefore, they were anxious for the UN's answer. UN would financially support everyone who was granted asylum. All had made a story based on the hope that the

UN would accept their claims. The UN officers, however, were skilled and experienced, and they wouldn't easily fall for it. There was a woven sign above the UN entrance with a picture of the Great Wall of China, under which asylum seekers would sit and wait for their name to be called. They would tell gorgeous stories under the picture of that great wall. Morteza, who had been nowhere to be seen, used to calm down the refugees' turbulent mind with his jokes and clownery.

Since his absence lasted long, the folks suggested inquiring after him from Amir shaleh[29] since he was *kaab-ol-akhbar.*[30] He was twenty-eight and lame, so his friends named him Amir Sholeh. He had told the UN that when in prison, he went lame after a bullet hit his leg, so his claim had not been dismissed. His close friends claimed that he was lying and had deceived the UN officers. They said he had been an electrician in Varamin, and he had fallen off the ladder and broken his leg. When they asked him where he had undergone surgery, he replied he had fled to Dubai and was operated there. They fell for it, and now he was well-off. He not only received money from the UN but also an Iranian widow, with whom he had got along, who paid for his expenses. He used to lie with her twice a week. Once, a folk who had recently been granted asylum gave a party at his home, where they asked him the whereabouts of Morteza. He

---

[29] Amir the Lame.

[30] Someone who has much information over many issues.

replied, "Don't worry. He's at his Thai girlfriend's place and lingering over there, warm and cozy."

A few days passed, and Morteza was still unaccounted for. After a while, the UN office heard about his absence. Ms. Tommy, the head of UN office for refugees, told the folks that they were waiting for Morteza. His claim was accepted, and he can find somewhere to rent out.

Amir heard it and immediately began his search. He asked the folks to get ready for a party, which Morteza was supposed to throw. "We should toss off a few bottles of Mekong (Thai liquor) by the Chao Phraya," he said. He took a took-took to visit Morteza's girlfriend. He rode to Bangabi Square and gave the driver a fifteen Baht fare. After the car chugged away, he limped along a street leading off the square and kept drying the sweats. It was boiling hot and muggy. Walking along the streets, he noticed some snake's skins sticking out from bushes. He pushed them inside the bushes to prevent the Thai children playing around in the streets from touching them. But a few steps ahead, he saw a small boy who was holding a live snake and winding it around his head, and he was saying something to other boys and girls in a language that Amir failed to understand. It came as a surprise to him how freaky and fearless they are.

Finally, he reached the compact house of Morteza's girlfriend, behind which was a swamp circled by wild trees and colorful flowers. He pressed the dislocated ring and waited for an answer. After a while, Morteza's girlfriend opened the door. Amir and Sou knew one another. Sou had a white flowered cloth around her body, which had left her chest and chubby white thighs naked.

Sou was a kind girl who usually wore a smile, a characteristic of Thai girls. Sou noticed the sweat streaming down Amir's face, so she invited him in immediately. Amir dried his face and stepped in. After he went into the room, he felt the coolness produced by an evaporative cooler whose generated stream was being circulated by a ceiling fan, and unintentionally, he said, "Ooh!"

Amir inquired after Morteza immediately after he got recovered. Sou did not say anything. She just took out two letters from a drawer of her dressing table and gave them to Amir. Then, in broken English, she said Morteza had left after he received the second letter, and she had not heard much of him since then. There was a one-and-a-half-month interval between the two letters. He wanted to read them right there, but he saw a young Thai boy coming into the room. He felt he had overstayed his welcome and left the house.

It was still hot. The scorching sunlight and the humid weather kept irritating everyone. First, he decided to read the letter in his own house, but he couldn't resist the impulse to read them under the sunlight. They had been sent by Morteza's family from Varamin. His mother wrote in the first letter:

> The grief I'm feeling over your absence is unbearable. Your father is sick and in desperate need of medication. I'm praying to God from

morning to night that your claim is accepted so that at least you can do something for us.

In the second letter, his younger brother wrote,

Where are you? Our mother is going to die from the grief of father who passed away last week.

Amir burst into tears afterward; his tears and sweat combined and turned too salty. He got worried more than ever. He was wondering where he could find him. Amir was about to lie with the widow that night, but he did not even call to tell her not to wait for him. He just rushed home and took out five hundred Baht he had hidden under the flooring. He left home to search for Morteza. He caught a taxi, a bus, and a took-took to get to different places where he thought Morteza might hang out. He found no trace of him though. Early in the morning, he got back home and fell asleep under the ceiling fan. He had a terrible nightmare. Suddenly he woke up and cursed the devil.

He sprung to his feet when he learned it was eleven thirty in the morning. He put on clothes and left home for the UN office. He thought the UN might ask the police for help. He visited Ms. Tommy at the UN office and gave the letters to her. He told her the whole story with a broken English and a bit of sign language. She was speechless and looked at him with grief. When Amir stopped speaking, Ms. Tommy gave Amir a crumbled paper. He got it with his shaking hand. He could guess what had happened from Tommy's expression. He hesitantly looked at the paper. It was Morteza's handwriting. He wrote,

My brother asked me where I am. Tell him "deep under the waters of Chao Phraya."

Thirst at the Seventh Station

THEY SAW ONE another as the train was departing the station. They were traveling in adjacent compartments. While standing by a window looking outside, they suddenly met one another's gaze, breaking into a smile as if they had been familiar with each other. After a while, the girl got back to her compartment, but the young boy stayed there. In his heart, he felt she would come back.

Hardly the train reached the next station when the girl left her compartment. When she saw the youth still standing at the window, she was delighted and gave him a smile.

They had already known each other's name before the train passed the second station. After the fifth one, they were eager to find an empty compartment to spend some time alone with no stranger's eyes out there.

At the seventh station, the train stopped for a few minutes. Some passengers got off, and some others went aboard. When it left the station, they both went to an empty compartment at the back of the train. A few lovely remarks were exchanged in a flash. They were about to experience the first kiss when the door opened and an old villager holding a red wooden suitcase appeared at the door.

Seeing the man, they had to release their grip on one another and stay back. The villager sat on the other side and stowed his suitcase under the seat. Sweat was pouring down his face. The man, whose clothes were loose, took a look at the boy and girl and then wiped his nose with a handkerchief. They didn't like the intruder, but they knew he meant no harm. Therefore, the girl came closer to the boy and tightened her hold on his hand.

The villager bent and took an onion out of his suitcase, peeking and biting it. Smell of onion filled the air, and the boy was looking surprisingly at the man who was eating it with an insatiable appetite. He noticed the surprised gaze of the young boy, and then he swiftly took out another onion and offered it to him.

"Here you are. It is good. Onion builds up your strength," he said.

The young boy was still silent, with his fingers rubbing smoothly the girl's fingers.

The villager could not get why the boy is staring at him. He kept offering him the onion, but the boy showed no reaction. He asked himself, *Why is the boy speechless and gazing at me?*

The train passed several other stations at short intervals. They were still holding one another's hands. It was enough to let flames of desire shoot further through them. The villager was still wondering why the young boy kept looking at him and remained silent.

Meanwhile, the train entered the tunnel, and the poorly lit space of the compartment turned dark. When it was leaving the tunnel, the villager's head was toward the window, so he didn't see they stopped kissing and moved their head backward.

The girl closed her eyes and glued her body to the boy. The man averted his eyes from the window and surprisingly noticed that the boy was still gazing at him. This time, he looked at the girl, who closed her eyes and was leaning against the boy.

"Your sister seems to be sick," the villager asked the boy.

The boy made no reply, and the villager took out another onion and offered it to them. "Give it to her. Onion is the remedy to all diseases."

The boy was still silent, staring at the villager's eyes.

After the tunnel, the two lovers moved their hands faster. The villager's mind kept wandering, and he was still wondering why the youth kept staring at him. He was growing angry and looking at the boy with an annoyed expression, telling himself, *Why the hell is he looking daggers at me?*

A few minutes later, the look of the boy was still glued to the confused villager. The man kept looking at the youth occasionally and averting his face again. Finally, he sprung to his feet and said, "I'm going out to drink water. I hope by the time I come back, you'll have found your tongue." The boy broke into a smile when the villager left the compartment. He was well aware that he would have enough time by the time the man got back. After all, the buffet car was in the middle of the train.

Naked in the Swamp

B ANAFSHEH LOOKED
OVER the window to get
familiar with the new place she was about to reside after
the Munich–Copenhagen train passed over the Adriatic
Sea and snaked out of the Princess Ship and into Danish
soil.

She was on the borderline in Turkey for two years
and went to great lengths in Munich for eight months
to make it to Denmark, where she had been told that
refugees are well treated, especially a deserted wife with
a baby.

It was uncharacteristically clear and sunny, satisfying
Danish people's craving for the sunlight.

The train was snaking on the Shinland's grasslands,
with Banafsheh still gazing out. Trees and grass were at
the edge of her vision. The earth was flat. There was no
bumpy terrain out there, but the bulges in her well-fit
body drew the attention of the officer who was there

to control the entry documents. He hit the door with a pen, and Banafsheh, who was standing by the window, turned her head. She was not worried as she had paid a smuggler five thousand dollars to help her cross the border with a Danish visa. The smuggler lived up to his promise properly. She received a warm welcome after the officer checked her documents and visa.

She headed toward the window. The train was travelling through a small residential area. A few houses were within sight. She saw some Danish women lying under the sun in the nude. Breaking unintentionally into a smile, she rubbed her face and chest, and then she began to touch lower parts, like a seller who is going to price his items.

At the same time, her daughter who was deeply asleep woke up suddenly, as though she had seen a nightmare. Then she turned around and got up. She first looked around. Her curious looks implied that she was looking for something. After failing to find it, she burst into tears. Banafsheh approached and hugged her. She wiped her tears while kissing her. The girl said, "Where is Father?"

Banafsheh replied, "I told you he will join us later, didn't I?"

She tightened her hold and said, "My sweet dream!"

Kissing her again, she carried her daughter toward the window and said, "Here is Denmark. You will grow up here." Then she uttered, "I can't stand his face anymore! There is no one sneakier than him." She began to fantasize as the four-year-old Roya was pacifying.

Banafsheh had recently got her bachelor's degree when she first met Iraj across the Tehran University's campus. They were busy debating over a critical issue when the revolutionary guards appeared at the scene, so the crowd dispersed. Iraj fled too, and then he approached a car whose driver was ready to pull out. Banafsheh was sitting at its wheel. His obtrusive entry outraged her. Iraj begged for help, describing the situation as a matter of life and death. It paved the way for their acquaintance and friendliness. Banafshed was stuck between a rock and a hard place too. She was well aware that if her belly bulged, she just had two options: she must either take her life, due to her parents' religion-based bigotry, or walk down the aisle with a man who had made her pregnant. The latter was impossible since Ahmed had told a lie to deceive her into lying with him. After a while, he left her behind. Three months later, he was reportedly seen in Denmark. Therefore, she had just one option: killing herself. She didn't have the guts though for she might have been sympathetic to the bastard baby she was expecting.

Banafsheh, who was first protesting Iraj's uninvited presence in her car, now began to develop a passion for him, feeling that she could have a heart-to-heart talk with another person in trouble. Therefore, she told her whole story. When she lightened up, Iraj took hold of her hand, ready to shift the gear.

"We'll flee as I know the way to do so,"

She was then filled with joy to an extent that she didn't notice that she'd got hold of his hand. At the same time, Iraj took great delight. His enjoyment was different from the one swept over Banafsheh over the likely escape from her family's bigotry.

It took one year and four months to slip into Turkey through a region bordering Azerbaijan. Banafsheh, who had suddenly disappeared before setting to Turkey, stayed in a country cottage near Maragheh; it belonged to a relative of Iraj. She gave birth to her daughter there. Iraj took good care of them because he really enjoyed lovemaking with Banafsheh, whose behavior was undergoing deep changes, uncharacteristic of an educated woman with a bachelor's degree. Bigotry, homelessness, lovemaking, escape, country life, and a bastard child had made her indifferent to life and the future. Sometimes the flames of revenge shot through her, which would subside soon. She had given up to momentary lapses.

When they arrived in Turkey, Iraj took her to a place in which he got the address from Tehran—a boarding house opposite the famous market of Istanbul; it was called the fugitive hotel. The house owner received their documents and gave them a room. After a week, Iraj disappeared. Banafsheh inquired after him, and the hotel owner said he would tell her the story that night.

The hotel owner approached Banafsheh at night. Then, she got familiar with his physique and feature for the first time. A thick black mustache had been placed under his hook nose. He had huge black eyes, and his well-developed body reminded her of *pahlavans*[31] of Tehran's old neighborhoods; however, in temperament, they were poles apart. His sensual look at her body

---

[31] Iranian athletes in the past who were famous for their strong body and chivalry

betrayed his feelings toward her. Banafsheh noticed his real feelings, so she asked for the whereabouts of Iraj. The Turkish man said, "Iraj is now in the United States, and you are at my disposal for a year to pay back the cost of his trip." She got to understand the trick she had fallen for and the unsympathetic world she got stuck in.

She was forced to go to bed with the Turkish man every night to pay for the costs of Iraj's trip. She also secretly had sex with others to save money for herself and her bastard daughter and set aside a little cash to save for their trip to Denmark.

The train was approaching Copenhagen, where Banafsheh changed it to travel to Helsingør. It was reportedly Ahmed's place of residence.

Less than two weeks into his residence, she was nicknamed Vyjayanthimala[32] by expatriate Iranians in Helsingør. She used to wear heavy makeup, putting on tight pairs of jeans in different colors, which displayed all her body bulges. She wore a white jacket, under which her chest was stuck out. Everybody gazed at her. All Iranians knew how whorish she was, but in a free country like Denmark, she was unlikely to come under attack. She was now a familiar sight. Some Danes gave her a hand to search for Ahmed; meanwhile, some frivolous Iranians didn't like Vyjayanthimala to find him.

After six months, all of a sudden, she got confined to her house as just leaving home to take Roya to the kindergarten or to go shopping. She didn't feel like

---

[32] An Indian famous star. Iranian men call a perverted woman Vyjayanthimala

wearing the clothes, posing her body, or putting on heavy makeup. Her change surprised everyone. It was just Roya who failed to notice all the events happening around her. She even didn't know her father had been found. One day, tired of playing in the yard, she walked toward her mother, only to find her lying on the ground. She struggled in vain to wake her up. She even knelt to shake her mother's body, but it was useless. Suddenly, she heard a noise from the door connecting the kitchen to the backyard, so she headed toward it. She didn't see anyone though. She even paid no attention to her knees stained with blood, which had been spurting out of her mother's back and spreading all over. She was a lonely, helpless girl who was drawn in the life swamp.

The Secret of Those
Black Eyes

I'M SITTING ON a rock, peering at the horizon off the Santa Barbara coast. The Pacific waters are unruffled, unlike what you might experience during stormy days. There is just a gentle breeze, letting me dispose of the heat produced by the direct sunlight. It is partially cloudy, with patches of clouds playing hide-and-go-seek with the sun.

There is a small camp inshore. I heard the water streaming down the showers. An old man is washing himself under a shower. A short distance away, a naked young woman is shampooing her hair. Under another shower, which is relatively close to me and next to the rocks, some small boys and girls are playing. The comings and goings is under way in some tents at the camp.

A flock of seagulls are flying overhead, one of which dives into the sea and catches a fish. Holding it with its beak, the bird flies toward a rock, where it settles triumphantly before trying to eat its prey. The fish slipped out of its beak though. Looking downward, the seagull seems to have no doubt it will be impossible to catch it again. Therefore, it flies off, with its face showing no sign of desperation.

Unintentionally, I turn down my face looking through the rocks. I feel the intuition that I might unexpectedly find something there. A whistle! It is a type of whistle referees use during matches. Looking downward, I notice it. It is not within reach though unless I pushed aside the rocks. Therefore, I have to leave it behind, as did the seagull. Unlike the bird, I have no feather to fly, but I want to visualize it. The bird might purposefully appear before me to fly me off. It catches the fish and leaves it behind, under the rocks, and then it turns its face down and have me follow suits.

The sky, the water, the seagull, and the breeze are all the same in nature, wherever they are. The people are exceptions though.

The seagull was able to provoke my imagination. The whistle also take me to the south coast of Iran, Bandar-e-Lengeh, with a bazaar, a school, a dirt track, dozens of compact houses, and a maze of streets.

Khadijeh used to sit at the far end of a street where Kamal's house was located with her black chador on. With her black veil always on, few people had seen her face. Her large eyes could be seen though. If someone gazed at her eyes over a few minutes, they would get enchanted. When her breasts jiggled under her chador, the wave of love and passion filled the air.

It was said that she had not seen her husband since the second day of her marriage. Some people said he had lingered in Dubai and got married afterward. Some others believed that he had been drowned. Khadijeh had to wait for him as her father had promised the groom to keep his daughter for him.

In the past few years, two bodies belonging to young men had been recovered from the sea; from then on, rumors went on that Khadijeh's husband had cursed them because of their affair with his wife. Therefore, no men felt like satisfying her burning desire. But seducers were all over the place.

Kamal was eighteen years old and famous for his whistle in Bandar-e Lengeh. Someone had brought him a whistle from Tehran as a souvenir. He blew it every day to kick off a football match on dirt grounds. Early in the morning, he headed toward the end of the street to buy a bowl of yogurt for his father. Khadijeh put earthen bowls of yogurt on a tray and walked toward the street where Kamal's house was located. She put it on the ground and passionately waited for Kamal.

When she saw his well-built body, she got delighted. Kamal paid attention to everything but Khadijeh. One day she took the plunge and unveiled her face, taking hold of Kamal's hand. He found how beautiful she was. His lips were ready to kiss her, and his eyes were glued to her. Khadijeh felt at loss, rising to her feet to face Kamal. She raised Kamal's hand, putting it on her breast. Now Kamal began to focus his attention on her, rubbing her large breasts and their upward nipples. Khadijeh's eyes became languid, so did those of Kamal.

From then on, Khadijeh would keep a low profile and wouldn't stand at the end of the street. In the street where Kamal lived, the cry of wail would be heard.

The inhabitants of Bandar-e Lengeh said that a few hours after he rubbed Khadijeh's breast and Khadijeh's eyes became languid, his corpse was recovered from the sea. His whistle was also found on a boat wandering on the waters without any passenger.

Twenty Years of
Expectation

T HE ELDERLY MAN struggled to move under the blanket and managed to rise to an upright position. When he sat, he hardly took several deep breaths. Then he tidied his long white hair, which had covered his shoulders. He also stroke his long gray beard. Taking another deep breath, he started to gaze at Mr. Eetezad Mozaffar. Mr. Eetezad was discreetly standing at the bed. He had a lorgnette on and wore a bright straw hat. Some drops of sweat were streaming down his face.

"This book is too dangerous," said the elderly man.

"You have stressed it several times, and you should be sure that I will keep it away from the wicked people," he said after he took off his hat and dried his sweat with a handkerchief.

The elderly man, who was still uncertain, bent and took out a casket whose capacity was enough for holding a book. Eetezad could hear his heart beating. The elderly man pushed the casket against his chest; it was covered with leather. Its color and sewing bore the testimony that it dated back to time immemorial. The man looked through a window facing the Mediterranean Sea. Old memories were being stirred in his mind.

He was born after his father left Cairo for Cyprus. He hadn't been in Tehran, but his parents had taught him how to speak Farsi. He was named Salman. His father was a literate man and had conducted numerous studies on the history of Egypt. He was also familiar with hieroglyphs, which was deciphered by French historian Champollion.

His father had given the casket to him upon his death. He was told that the casket contained a book written during the time of pharaohs, the period in which Memphis served as the political capital of Egypt and the Giza pyramid complex was constructed at the order of pharaoh known as Cheops and Iranians took over the book, which had been kept in the tomb of a pharaoh's wife, after they conquered Egypt; from then on, only god knows who had been in possession of it.

Salman was still on a trip down memory lane, refusing to release his tight hold on the casket. Meanwhile, Mr. Eetezad said, "Salman Khan! The ship will leave in an hour. If I fail to catch it, I have to stay in Cyprus for another three weeks."

Salman Khan recovered his senses and said, "That's right, but I will repeat my request. Do not open it unless you find the pair of the book."

Mr. Eetezad, who was ready to leave, said, "Luckily, as your father advised, we have followed the clues and have no doubt that the pair of this book is in Tripoli. Upon my arrival to Tehran, I will leave it in a secure place and plan a trip to Tripoli. I will let you in on it."

"If I won't have passed the buck by then," said the old man desperately, while still looking at the Mediterranean Sea.

The elderly man gave the casket to Mr. Eetezad unwillingly, as if he was yielding to the Grim Reaper.

Mr. Eetezad Mozaffar took over the casket in satisfaction and gave six wads of Cyprus pound to the man. The elderly man threw them on the bed indifferently though. He said, "This book is priceless. The money is useless for my life too. I will spend it on the maintenance of this library to make eternal the name of Iran on the island, a country that I have never visited."

Mr. Eetezd Mozaffar kept a tight hold of the casket as he left the stony house of the elderly man located on the library roof. He stepped down the stairs. The library was on the top of a hill, on the skirt of which was a village. Hundreds of books, some paintings, and an old statue were being kept there. Less than half of the books had been brought from Iran.

There was a donkey fastened to a tree in front of the building. He left the library and approached the donkey. As he was mounting it, he took a look at the sign of the library, the name of which was Salman. Mr. Eetezad Mozaffar unfastened the rope at the donkey's neck, and it started to walk down along the cobbled street joining the library to the village.

It was one in the afternoon on a hot summer day in 1960, when Cyprus was in a state of elation at the independence from Britain. People were dancing and feasting in celebration of their freedom from Britain. You could see delight in the face of all Cypriots. Orthodoxies and Muslims were performing ceremonial dances to the music being played by the buskers. Deep in his heart, he could feel an uproar. It was quite different from that of Cypriots though. Following years of conducting research and spending huge amount of money, he had acquired a treasure, whose missing pair was to be unearthed; otherwise, his attempt would be futile, and the first pair might cause serious harm.

He was in a state of considerable agitation from the time he boarded a ship sailing to Turkey to the time he caught a plane flying to Tehran. His mind was hovering around the old libraries of Tripoli he had conducted research on.

He stood on the deck, gazing at the full moon. He uttered, "The moon knows everything, but regretfully, it is dumb and just looking down." He sat on a bench and lighted a cigarette. He took a puff and, after exhaling the smoke, said, "It took twenty years to find the book. If it takes twenty good years to find its pair, I would turn sixty. I would have enough time to divulge the secrets of the pharaoh's beautiful wife."

At the time, the Nicosia ship was sailing through the Mediterranean Sea under the moonlight and approaching Turkey.

Two days later, the Homa Airline's flight 322 landed on the Mehrabad Airport. Mr. Eetezad Mozaffar made a quick exit. He had no baggage to collect. He just had a handbag, which he was keeping tight hold of. It contained the casket, so nobody could pay attention to it.

A 1959 black Chevrolet was waiting for him at the airport. The chauffeur got out of the car as he saw Mr. Eetezad Mozaffar. He bent and opened the door. Mr. Eetezad got in, and the driver pulled away. It was ten minutes to seven in the afternoon. Looking at his watch, he inquired after his son. He asked, "Where is Jamshid?"

"He has gone to the birthday party of Shokat-ol-Muluk Khanum's daughter. He inquired after you too. I told him the prince is still in Cyprus. I didn't know you would return so early."

Mr. Eetezad took a look inside the bag to make sure the casket is still there. Pressing it against his chest, he said, "I'm in a hurry. I should travel to Tripoli."

The driver tried to charm his master and said, "You get exhausted by these trips."

Mr. Eetezad rubbed the bag and replied, "It is worthwhile."

The clock struck two. Mr. Eetezad was still sitting at his desk, looking through several old books on the pharaohs and ancient history of Egypt.

The casket was on the desk too. He kept looking at it regularly. He stroked the leather cover of the casket several times and glued his gaze to its lock. It didn't have any key, but the secret to unlocking it was written next to the lock.

Jamshid got home twenty minutes after two in the morning. He was intoxicated and staggering toward his room. Suddenly, he noticed the light streaming from his father's room. Heading to the room, he saw his father studying at his desk. He greeted his father, who got joyful after seeing him. Jamshid was joyful too. His father asked, "Did you have a good time?"

"I had a great time," he replied. "If you had been there, I would be through with it. Shokat-ol-Muluk Khanum's daughter confessed that she is in love with me."

His father said, "It was clear from the very beginning. But you should wait. After all, women have many secrets. You should learn them all step-by-step. This makes your life easier."

"But I love her," he replied and added, "I can't wait anymore."

His father said, "Don't be so candid. You must take lessons from me."

He put his hand on the casket and went on, "I spent twenty years of my life to discover the secrets of a beautiful Egyptian woman."

Jamshid burst into laughter and said, "You're lucky my mother is not alive."

His father paid no attention to him and went on, "If it takes a further twenty years, it is not a matter of importance. Now I possess the most valuable treasure in the world, and I will acquire more in the future."

Jamshid was too drunk to understand what his father was saying. Drinking alcohol had made him tactless, so he could easily talk to his father, but he didn't know what he meant. He said good-night consciously or unconsciously and went upstairs to sleep.

The clock struck four. Mr. Eetezad Mozaffar, who felt exhausted, left his desk and headed toward his bedroom. A few minutes later, his luxurious house was dominated by sheer silence. The casket was left on the desk too.

Jamshid was lying prone on the bed. He suddenly turned and partly opened his eyes. He couldn't resist the thirst followed by drinking alcohol and get up to go to the kitchen for a glass of water. He drank water and shuffled toward his bedroom again. While passing his father's room, he suddenly noticed his desk. He saw the casket and remembered the remarks of his father. Curiously, he walked toward it.

Half an hour later, Jamshid was in his room and had trouble sleeping. Lying on the bed, he was staring at the ceiling. He was thinking about Shokat-ol-Muluk Khanum's daughter. All of a sudden, a silhouette distracted his attention. He first assumed that he had been hallucinating. A few seconds later, he had no doubt that a young lady was approaching him. The woman, whose scent had filled the room, broke into a smile. Her makeup and dressing style suggested that she was a pharaoh's wife. Hardly had he said a word when she knelt before him. She put off the fine green silk fabric covering her marbled body. Her breasts were shaking, and her thighs sparked in the darkness. Her big black eyes were filled with passion, and her face began to light up. All of a sudden, she jumped at Jamshid, and both began to shag.

Mr. Eetezad Mozaffar woke up to a direct sunlight touching his face. He jumped to his feet after recovering consciousness. It was ten. He rushed to his room. He got into a panic when he saw his room. He was faced with a broken casket and scattered papers. Some odd pictures had illustrated them, and illegible words had been put down.

Overwhelmed by horror, he bent over to pick up the papers. Suddenly, he heard a moan. He listened carefully and felt that someone was asking for help. It struck more terror into his heart. He left the papers behind to follow the noise. It came from his son's room. Stepping upstairs, he reached the room. Opening the door, he faced an old man who seemed to be a thousand years old. A shiver ran through him. Gazing at him, he managed to identify his son despite numerous wrinkles covering his face. Jamshid was not able to talk and move. He hardly stretched his hand toward his father and said, "Father! Help me!"

Not long afterward, Mr. Eetezad Mozaffar erupted into shouting and lapsed into unconsciousness. One day later, he became conscious, but he had lost his sanity. He was taken by ambulance to the hospital.

A Whirlwind Romance
at the Seaside

THEY FIRST MET one another on the train heading for *Hamburg*. Sohrab boarded the train in Munich. Nobody had accompanied Sohrab to see him off, so unlike other passengers, he didn't stand at the corridor and went straight to his compartment, which was still empty. He first threw his bag on the seat, under which he carefully stowed his violin. Then he put his bag in front of it to protect the instrument from any impact.

Passengers began to go to their compartments when the train left the station. Two stout couples entered the compartment in which Sohrab was sitting; they had rosy cheeks and had knitted sweaters on. A few minutes later, a tall man wearing a black raincoat joined them. The couples sat across Sohrab, and the tall man sank into the same seat, leaving just a little space between him and Sohrab. All were German, characteristically serious and quiet. The tall man immediately rested his head on the angle between the seat back and the compartment wall. The stout couples opened a pocket of raisins and began eating them.

Sohrab was scrutinizing them. When he learned that the couples did not pay any attention to him, he took out his music pocket notebook from his jacket. He took a look at the notes and started to whistle a recently self-composed piece of music. Although he was not too noisy, the woman threw a harsh look at Sohrab as a protest. Sohrab stood and immediately left the compartment. Before he left, he said "Idiot!" in Farsi.

When Sohrab entered the corridor, he faced a girl sitting on her suitcase by the window. The girl, who didn't have warm clothes on, was shivering with cold. Sohrab put his notebook into his pocket and walked toward her. Her olive skin indicated that she was not a German. He wanted to ask her where she was from, but he aborted his question after he noticed that the girl was reading a book in Farsi. He learned that she was his compatriot.

They spent over two hours in the buffet car. Anyone who saw them for the first time assumed that they had been familiar with one another for ages. Living in exile seemed to have made them draw near. They felt like speaking loudly in their mother tongue to annoy the racist German.

Sohrab, who knew the girl's name by then, told her that "Germans treat refugees kindly in the camp, but as soon as someone leaves there, they start to look down on him." The young girl, Mitra, told him that immigration officers had given her hell at the airport. The two young passengers were heading for Hamburg to wait for an answer from the immigration office at the major camp.

Emotionally, they became closer to one another as time was passing at the camp. They had been brought together. When Sohrab was playing the violin, Mitra felt she was a diver swimming deep into the sea. Upon the end of any piece of music, she held his hand and kissed his fingers. Sohrab, who had the time of his life, stroked her hair. A kiss from her lips would revive him as if he had drunk the fountain of youth. Their love story had become well-known. Everyone had heard Sohrab's violin tone. Mitra's story had yet to be heard by Sohrab though. He had tried in vain to learn where she had come from and what made her so dismayed. He could easily feel her agitation any time she heard footsteps or a screech of brakes. He had tried to elicit a response from the girl, but she kept playing her cards close to her chest. Her secretiveness annoyed Sohrab a lot.

Once, they left the camp for the sea. They stayed there by dusk. Then they lighted a fire. Watching the flickering flames, they leaned against one another. As he pulled the bow across the string, she burst into tears. Their love story came to an end before the end of the piece.

The next morning, Sohrab was found unconscious in a pool of blood by the sea. The fire had gone out, and the violin was broken. The tracks of a vehicle and some footsteps had been left behind.

The following morning, a piece of news hit the headlines of Hamburg's morning papers, reporting a car crash in which notorious smugglers of women and a young girl who had fallen prey to them were killed.

Shila

THE VILLA AT the seaside was so quiet that a pin drop could be heard. Silence had fallen upon the salon and rooms, although they had witnessed numerous memories. The sea was dead calm too. There was just a banging noise made after a gentle breeze from the sea hit a mesh screen door. Conversely, Shila and Behruz lying on the glossy sand by the sea were not making any noise. There was just silence, but they felt a commotion in their mind that had made them agitated.

Shila asked herself whether Behruz was the man she was dreaming of. And Behruz hopefully expected that Shila's father would lend him $100,000 he needed desperately.

Shila felt like talking more about love, and she wanted to make sure that Behruz would belong to her forever. Conversely, Behruz was pondering on another future. He had claimed if she helped him to inject that amount of money into his Mexican firm, there would be no concern over the future.

It took her a few weeks to talk her father into lending the money to Behruz.

Her family, highly reputed and immensely wealthy, would introduce Behruz as an economic figure, and Shila would tell her friends that, from the time he stepped into her life, she hadn't even thought of the smartest Hollywood stars. She would claim that Behruz had the key to her heart and nobody could open it except for him. Meanwhile, Behruz thought of love differently. He was just anxious to receive the $100,000, by which he could meet his goal. All in all, he had given love the second priority.

Shila's father finally deposited $100,000 in his daughter's account. From then on, Behruz was able to realize his ambition. He kissed and praised Shila to the skies. Surprised by his passionate reactions, she likened her beloved to kids for his manner. Having broken into smile, she asked him, "What's wrong with you, Behruz? I didn't know $100,000 can cheer you up. Otherwise, I'd have asked my father for it earlier."

They were in the car a few hours later, and Behruz was heading downtown, where there were no wealthy and well-reputed citizens.

Out of concern, Shila asked, "Where are you going? It's dangerous here. Gangs might attack us. They will damage my car."

Behruz pulled in in front of a decrepit house, which barely had a chance to stand by the following winter. He told Shila that he would come back soon.

Shila, who was scared, said, "I'm frightened." Behruz, who was out of control over the joy of the acquired money, replied, "I told you once I should go there alone. You insisted on coming. You don't need to be worried. I will be here soon. I should help a poor man who used to be my worker."

Behruz immediately got out and walked toward the desolate house. As he entered, a four-year-old girl and an eight-year-old boy cheerfully approached him. They kept shouting "Dad! Dad!" Behruz hugged his kids and sniffed at them as if they were flowers. He said, "Now your mother has a lawyer to defend her. I'll spend that sum of money to guarantee her freedom. She is innocent."

As he was shedding tears and kissing his kids, he added, "If that monster hadn't been killed, he would have raped her. My wife is not a killer. If his head hadn't struck against the table, he wouldn't have been killed. We have a god after all."

All of a sudden, the kids set eyes on a woman standing by the broken door and listening to them. She was nobody but Shila.

Northbound and Southbound Trains

THE YOUNG MAN cleaned the chairs and tables of the seaside nightclub and approached a man sitting at the counter. He was taking puffs on his cigarette.

There was a bottle of vodka and an empty glass in front of him. There was a little vodka in the bottle, enough to fill a glass. He could still take further puffs at his cigarette. The young man wanted to dispose of him soon. If he was held up by the man, he would miss the train he was waiting for, and he had to wait for the following one. On the other hand, he didn't feel like intruding upon the man's complex and quiet solitude. He seemed to be in his midfifties. However, his thick white hair, which he kept stroking with his fingers, indicated that it had turned white prematurely.

The wrinkles on his forehead and creases on his face suggested a pain harming him from inside.

Before he reached the man, he changed his direction and went to take the broom. Then he started to sweep the floor. The man took another deep puff at his cigarette and stubbed it out on the ashtray. He breathed some fresh air in. For another time, he opened a small notebook and gazed at a picture belonging to a woman, saying, "Finally, I'll find her." He sighed deeply and picked up the vodka bottle. He poured its content completely into his glass and, as he was swinging it smoothly, stared at a point. Then he drank it up at one go.

The young man kept watching him while sweeping. The man left the glass on the counter, which he later put his head on, as if he couldn't resist its weight. It seemed that he liked it there and felt like sleeping over. The young man ran toward him after he saw the action, saying, "Sir! I have to close here. If you hurry up, I will catch the first train heading south."

The man, who raised his head, said, "I should catch the train heading north too. I dreamed that I have found the missing person I'm looking for there."

The man stood to his feet and pulled out his billfold from his back pocket. He took a bill out of his billfold and gave it to the young man. The young man went to another room to change the bill. But when he came back, the man had left. As he disappeared, the young man felt unconsciously that he had missed someone. Meanwhile, he heard the train whistle. He immediately looked at the clock and said, "It is the north train, and a few minutes later the south train departs too." Then he went to find the keys. Suddenly the notebook, which had been left behind by the man, grabbed his attention. He wanted to get to the man in order to give it to him, but it was too late. After all, the northbound train had blown its whistle three times. He opened the notebook to find a telephone or address. He did so only to get stunned after he saw the picture belonging to the woman. It was quite similar to the one he kept in his pocket. He took his billfold out and opened it. He made a comparison between them and found them totally similar. As the young man said "How did he get my mother's photo?" the southbound train blew its whistle. But his attention had been just focused on the man he deeply felt his absence, and all of a sudden, he felt he had a missing person to look for.

Spending a Friday with Gina Lollobrigida[33]

---

[33] Gina Lollobrigida is an Italian actress.

IT WAS FRIDAY. High streets in Shiraz would be teeming with a huge crowd on Fridays, when people could watch two movies with a single ticket in the morning and in the evening. Hamid was among the audience crowding out of Cinema Metro after the movie came to an end. He felt like eating something, and the tantalizing smells of fried dishes lingering in the air were about to tempt him into making his way into a food outlet to order a sandwich and his favorite beer, Argo. All of a sudden, he recalled that his mother was awaiting him at home to serve him shami kebab for lunch.

Hamid went home on foot. His house was within a striking distance of Shahpur High School. The destination was not a matter of concern though. He had fallen in love with Gina Lollobrigida, with whom the Hunchback of Notre Dame was in love too. Any film featuring Gina Lollobrigida would attract Hamid to the cinema at its premiere. When he left the cinema, he would prefer to walk all the way home to have enough time to think about her.

As he reached the house, he walked toward the a smal Basin to wash his face. Meanwhile, he shouted and called his mother,

"I got back. I'm starving to death, so waste no time in making the food ready."

His mother rushed out of the room and, at the point of her finger, tried to make him understand something. "Watch your behavior," she said quietly and added, "We have guests."

He replied, "What was wrong with my behavior? Anyway. Who are they?"

"New neighbors," she answered.

As Hamid got to the drawing room, he saw a woman veiling herself modestly from head to toe, who was in the company of a young boy and two relatively older girls.

Hamid greeted her, and after she turned her face toward him, he got stunned. She bore a striking resemblance to Gina Lollobrigida. It was so striking that Hamid couldn't help explaining it. But his mother made a sharp retort and said, "Watch your language. She is Jaleh Khanum, whose husband is Haj Agha Pineh Duz, who has an outlet out in the street."

Hamid was still stunned by that resemblance, so he couldn't understand what she said. Jaleh Khanum broke into a smile, and then let her hair and chest appear under her chador and said, "It's very kind of you." Meanwhile, Hamid's heart started to pound, strong enough to be heard by Jaleh Khanum.

The following morning, Haj Agha Pineh Duz rented two rooms in the same house for his Gina Lollo-like young wife and his three kids. From then on, her wife barely missed a chance to stay out, and Hamid didn't feel like watching Gina Lollobrigida's movies. Jaleh Khanum now knew the Hunchback of Notre Dame by heart.

A Cup of Black Coffee

HE GAVE HER mother a brush-off and stormed toward the door. He opened the door angrily to rush out of the house. He heard his mother's voice from behind. She was expressing her feelings in a furious manner; a trace of kindness was being felt in her voice though. She said, "What I say is for your own good, that's why I tell you that girl is not suitable for you."

The ignorant son slammed the door and headed toward his car. He got into the vehicle, pulled out, and pedaled furiously away.

For a while, he was wandering the streets. He was ignoring the traffic lights, but he survived several car crashes. In spite of that, his car was still rolling along fast, and he didn't feel like slowing down. Luckily, a police officer stopped his car and gave him a ticket for speeding; otherwise, his furiousness might cost him dearly. He was stopped in front of a café. After he received his ticket, he stormed into the café. A beautiful girl working there appeared at his table to take his order. He ordered a black coffee.

The girl, who noticed his anger, went to make his order ready.

The boy dialed a number with his cell phone. A girl answered his call, saying, "Did you talk to your mother?"

"Yes," he replied.

"What did she say?" the girl asked.

He said, "The usual remarks. She doesn't like you."

"I told you she is jealous of me," she answered. "Now that we are yet to get married, she wants to give me orders. Let alone the time we get married. She would consider me as her waitress. I've gotten insane for her words."

"I've gotten crazy too," the boy said. "I can't get along with her anymore."

Meanwhile, the girl approached him with a cup of coffee and said joyfully, "Are you sure you don't want sugar in your coffee? Your face is bitter enough."

The boy took an interrogative look at her and said, "No thank you."

The girl left him, and the other girl on the phone said, "Who the hell are you flirting with?"

He retorted, "Don't you start nagging again. I'm here for a coffee. I was in a temper and driving like a maniac, so a police fined me."

She said, "It's your mother's fault, she made you crazy. Any what are you going to do now?"

"I've decided to leave home forever," he replied. "I'll rent a room, and the uncertainty will come to an end."

"I agree too. It's better for both of us." She added, "It's a pity I'm not OK. Otherwise, I would be with you. Doctor has advised me I should get enough rest. He claimed your mother's despotic behavior had got on my nerves."

He said, "Don't irritate yourself, honey! Everything will be all right, we love one another, which is a matter of importance."

She said, "I love you. Come to my place tomorrow. I'll be missing you till tomorrow."

"I'll see you tomorrow."

After the phone call came to an end, he broke into a smile, and his bitter face lightened up a bit.

Half an hour passed. He left the café and got a bouquet of carnations at a florist's, which was within a striking distance. Then he got into the car and uttered, "It is the first anniversary of our friendship, and I should surprise her." A while later, he parked his car in front of the girl's house, wearing a perfume that he used to keep in the dashboard. He tidied his hair and left the car while carrying the bouquet.

He headed toward the room where the girl lived and then knocked at the door. He also covered the peephole with a finger to prevent the girl from looking through it. The girl answered the door and said, "Who are you?"

The boy changed his voice and said,

"Express parcel post!"

The girl, who had just covered her body with a sheet, opened the door with hesitation. Suddenly, the boy shouted, "Surprise!"

The girl screamed unintentionally, and then a man who was in the same room anxiously asked, "What's up, honey?"

From then on, no voice was heard. Just a black coffee smell that filled the air.

Darya

HE WAS IN a foul temper when he got home. He lay on the bed with his clothes still on.

Silence had ascended upon the coastal town. Except for the sound of the sea, no other noise was being heard; it was created when the waves broke on the shore.

His compact house stood in the vicinity of the sea, and he was agitated, like the waves. He kept tossing and turning all night; being frustrated, he left the bed and stepped toward the window. He opened the window, and the waves made their presence felt. He seemed to have been pacified by them. Standing by the window, he lighted a cigarette and started to draw on it. He took the first puff and blew the smoke into the air. The sea seemed to be talking to him. He began to talk to the sea too. He was under the illusion that the sea had fallen in love with him. He took another puff on the cigarette and told the sea that his significant other has an advantage over it, endowed with a nice face and long hair. Her name was Darya.

Ali couldn't believe he might fall in love again after bidding farewell to the capital and started to reside in a coastal town to leave behind his bittersweet past.

He first met her in the bazaar. Ali went there to buy fish. She was there in the company of her mother. The storekeepers treated them with great respect, so Ali was curious to know why. Ali asked a storekeeper who they were after they got into a car whose chauffeur had been waiting for them. He replied, "They are the family of a man who manages the town's woody plant."

Ali had just started his life in a strange town where he knew nobody. He didn't feel like developing an acquaintance in the town. Ali, who was still struggling with his past, would spend the nights by the seashore. He had been seeking employment. Once, he had applied for a job in the woody plant. As a skilled accountant, he managed to find a job there.

As time passed, Ali got familiar with the workflow after he studied the records and tried hard to knock the company into shape. Some workers and some outsiders warned him that, before he began to work seriously, he'd better get familiar with the wild side of the manager and know what lay behind that deceptive appearance.

He failed to heed them though, but one day, the turning point came.

It was night. Ali was strolling on the beach and pondering over his past. All of a sudden, a car screeched to a halt. Consequently, he heard a woman screaming blue murder. Ali approached the noise and noticed two shadows behind the rocks. He rushed to them and saw a villager gagging a woman and struggling to lay her on the ground; another man was unfastening his belt. It provoked Ali's reaction, so he shouted at them. Therefore, the two men, who had covered their faces, ran off.

He walked toward the woman and, under the moonlight, found Darya half-naked. Darya, the daughter of the man who managed the plant, was now broken like Venus de Milo and was reflecting the moonlight. Ali covered her body immediately and took her to his house. He switched the light on. He couldn't take his eyes off her worried face. Although there was a look of sheer terror on her face, she was still charming. He had carried her from the beach to his house, and he could still enjoy her body warmth. She gave Ali a distinct impression while laid on the bed. There was nothing but lingering silence and lasting looks. Emotions were stirring inside them as they gazed at one another.

The following morning, rumor had it that the manager's daughter had innocently fallen victim to the sexual assaults of her father.

It grieved Darya and her mother to hear such things. The manager was trying to change the public's opinion in his favor. Ali was lending him a hand too. The warmth of Darya's body had driven Ali into favoring her father over the others, so he kept making a stand against rumors.

His behavior didn't sit well with the workers, one of whom once told him, "The men who were about to assault Darya were the father and brother of a girl who is employed by the company. The manager had once threatened the girl with dismissal and then raped his victim." Ali didn't find what others said acceptable. After all, he loved Darya.

Two weeks later, a worker died after suffering from a chronic disease for a long time. The manager held a fabulous funeral for him and arranged for an impressive ceremony. He also offered his family members a generous financial help.

When some colleagues provided Ali with the poor man's medical record, he learned that the man had asked for sick leave several times, but the manager had not granted it. At last, his condition worsened, and following backbreaking work, he passed away.

He began to learn that the great funeral had been aimed at winning the hearts and minds of the workers and shifting public opinion in favor of the manager.

Ali was now stuck between a rock and a hard place. He had fallen hopelessly in love with Darya.

Darya was head over heels in love with Ali too. Ali was smart and attractive to her; she also found him enchanting and captivating, so she was determined not to lose him at any price.

He took another look at the sea. He put out his cigarette stub and sank into the bed again. He kept tossing and turning several times, and finally, he fell asleep.

The following morning, he woke up to the banging sound of the casements hitting their frame. He walked toward the window and looked through it. A fresh breeze was touching his face. It was high noon. He didn't feel like going to the factory. He felt like sitting down and looking at a picture he had drawn of Darya.